Best Book of Fairy Tales

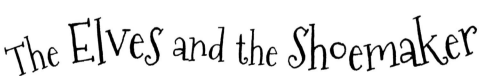

MILES
KELLY

First published in 2018 by Miles Kelly Publishing Ltd
Harding's Barn, Bardfield End Green, Thaxted, Essex, CM6 3PX, UK

This edition printed 2018

2 4 6 8 10 9 7 5 3

Publishing Director Belinda Gallagher
Creative Director   Jo Cowan
Editorial Director   Rosie Neave
Senior Editor Amy Johnson
Design Manager Simon Lee
Senior Designer Rob Hale
Cover Designer Joe Jones
Production Elizabeth Collins, Jennifer Brunwin-Jones
Reprographics Stephan Davis, Jennifer Cozens
Assets Lorraine King

ISBN 978-1-78617-523-6

Printed in China

British Library Cataloguing-in-Publication Data
A catalogue record for this book is available from the British Library

ACKNOWLEDGEMENTS
The publishers would like to thank the following artists who have contributed to this book:
Jack and the Beanstalk: Claudia Ranucci (Plum Pudding)
The Elves and the Shoemaker: Maxine Lee (The Bright Agency)
The Ugly Duckling: Agurtzane Abajo (Astound)
The Three Billy Goats Gruff: Marcela Calderón (Advocate Art)

Made with paper from a sustainable forest

www.mileskelly.net

Jack and the Beanstalk

Jack and his mother were very poor.

Market

Town

One day, Jack's mother said to him, "You must take the cow to market and sell her." They needed money to buy food.

Jack hadn't gone far when he met an old man who offered to swap **five beans** for the cow.

"Why would I do that?" asked Jack.

"These beans are magic. Plant them at night and by morning they will have grown right up to the sky."

So Jack took the beans and went home.

6

Jack's mother was furious.
"You've been tricked!" she cried, as she
threw the beans out of the window.

She sent Jack
to bed without
any supper.

In the morning, Jack looked outside in amazement. A huge **beanstalk** had grown – it went up and up, and up!

The beans really were **magic!**

8

Jack quickly got dressed. "I'm going on an adventure," he told his mother.

9

He began to climb the beanstalk.

When at last he reached the top, he saw a magnificent house sitting on a cloud.

Jack knocked on the door, and a giantess opened it.

"I suppose you're hungry after all that climbing," she said. "Come in and have some breakfast."

11

Hastily, Jack hid. He peeked out to see a HUGE giant stomp into the kitchen.

"FEE FI FO FUM, I smell the blood of an Englishman!"

13

The giant searched but couldn't find Jack, so he ate a huge breakfast, then started to count his gold.

He soon fell fast asleep.

14

Jack snatched a bag of gold
and dashed out of the house
and down the beanstalk.

His mother was
so pleased to
see him. And now
they had money
for food!

15

The next day, Jack climbed the beanstalk again. The giantess let him in, and her husband was soon home. Again, Jack hid.

"FEE FI FO FUM, I smell the blood of an Englishman!"

After his breakfast,
the giant placed a
golden hen
on the table.

"Lay, hen!" he ordered, and the
hen started laying golden eggs.

17

When the giant fell asleep, Jack snatched the hen and climbed down the beanstalk.

His mother was delighted.

18

Jack climbed the beanstalk
again the next day.
He crept into
the house.

He knew the giantess
would not have let
him in again.

19

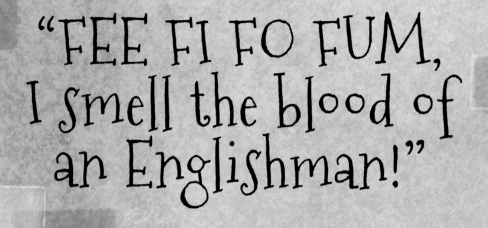

"FEE FI FO FUM, I smell the blood of an Englishman!"

The giant was home, but he couldn't find Jack anywhere, so he sat down and ate an even bigger breakfast.

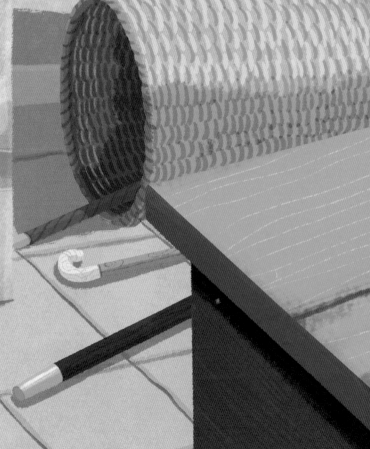

20

Then the giant placed a golden harp on the table. "Play, harp!" he said.

The harp began playing a beautiful lullaby. Soon the giant was snoring.

21

Jack snatched the harp
and raced out of the
house and back down
the beanstalk.

But the harp called,
"Master, master!"
and the giant woke up.

The giant chased Jack
down the beanstalk.
"FEE FI FO FUM!
I SMELL THE
BLOOD OF AN
ENGLISHMAN!"

23

As Jack reached the bottom, he ran to fetch an axe.

He chopped and chopped until...

24

CRASH!

The giant was flung far away, and Jack never saw him again.

The beanstalk tumbled to the ground.

Jack and his mother lived happily ever after, and were never poor again.

The Elves and the Shoemaker

Once upon a time, a shoemaker and his wife had the **busiest shoe shop** in town.

Even **the king himself** had been known to visit from time to time.

But the shoemaker's shoes went **out of fashion** and he grew poor.

One evening, he only had enough leather left to make **one more pair.**

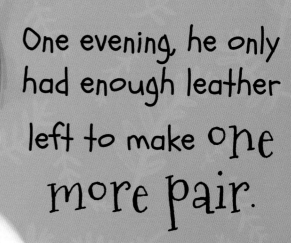

"I'll sew this together in the morning," he said to his wife.

"Once these shoes are made and sold, who knows what will happen to us."

And they went to bed.

Next morning, the shoemaker was **amazed** to see a pair of shoes quite finished on his bench.

He blinked in surprise and called for his wife.

32

The shoes were **so neatly made** that the stitches could barely be seen.

The shoemaker put the shoes in the window and opened up. He didn't have long to wait before a customer came in to try the shoes on.

34

The woman bought the shoes for a good price. The shoemaker couldn't believe his **luck**.

Now he had the money to buy enough leather for two more pairs of shoes!

35

That night, the shoemaker **cut out the leather**, ready to sew in the morning.

But the next day, there were two pairs of shoes already made – and every bit as fine as the pair before.

There were customers waiting outside, too. News had spread about the first **beautiful** pair of shoes.

The two new pairs sold in seconds.

The shoemaker was able to buy more leather, and every day more shoes were made. Never had the shop been so busy! People came from far and wide.

The shoemaker had to take on an assistant to help serve customers. Soon he and his wife were rich.

One evening, the shoemaker said to his wife, "Why don't we stay up and see if we can spot who makes the shoes?"

42

The shoemaker's wife thought it was a great idea. They left the light on in the workshop and hid behind a curtain.

43

At midnight, two tiny elves crept into the workshop. They wore ragged clothes and caps.

They sat at the workbench and began to stitch, sew and hammer.

44

They were so skilful and quick.

45

The next morning the shoemaker's wife said, "Those little elves have made us rich, We must thank them. Did you see how ragged their clothes were?"

46

"I'll make new little shirts and coats, and vests and trousers, and you make two tiny pairs of shoes." So that is what they did.

47

A few nights later, they laid their **Presents** on the workbench and hid behind the curtain.

At midnight, the elves appeared – how happy they were to find their **new outfits!**

48

They put them on and danced about. Then the two little elves skipped away into the night...

and the shoemaker and his wife never saw them again.

But they didn't mind, because they now had enough money to **stop work for good.**

They both lived happily ever after.

The Ugly Duckling

One sunny spring day when the countryside was covered in blossom, a duck was sitting on her **nest** on the bank of a river.

She was getting fed up of waiting for her eggs to hatch. At last, the shells began to crack, one after another.

"Peep, Peep!" chirped the little ducklings.

"Quack, quack!" said mother duck.

54

"Oh dear, there's one egg left," mother duck sighed.

She settled back down on the nest to wait.

55

A few days later, the big egg
did at last **crack**. Out tumbled...
a very different-looking duckling!

"Peep!"

Mother duck was very surprised. The last duckling was big, and grey, and rather... Ugly.

"Never mind, I shall treat him just the same as the rest."

The next day, mother duck proudly led her family along the river and into the duck yard.

When the other ducks saw the big grey duckling they hissed, "What is that ugly-looking thing? We don't want him around here."

Mother duck tried to protect her strange little one, but everyone said he **didn't belong** in the duck yard.

Every day, the ugly duckling was pushed about and made fun of by all the other ducks.

Even his brothers and sisters began to be nasty to him.

60

So he ran away.

One day, he just sprang
up into the air and
dropped over the fence.

The ugly duckling ran until he reached a marsh. The wild ducks there all agreed that he was terribly ugly, but they said he could stay.

62

"As long as you keep your distance!"

He spent his days swimming on the marsh and diving down in it for food.

No one spoke to him.
No one cared about
him. He was very
lonely.

63

Weeks went by. One evening, a flock of birds appeared. They were **dazzling white,** with long graceful necks.

The duckling crouched among the reeds and watched – he had never seen birds so beautiful.

64

They soared up into the sky.
As the duckling watched them
go, he longed to be with them.

Winter arrived, and the marsh became so icy that the duckling nearly froze.

He kept himself going with the thought of seeing those magnificent birds again.

"Brrrrrrr!"

66

Then one day,
the warm SUN of
springtime shone.

Before the ugly duckling quite
knew what was happening, he
found himself flapping his wings
and taking to the air.

67

After a while, he landed in a river that wound through a beautiful garden.

Three graceful birds were
swimming towards him.

69

The ugly duckling bowed his head,
waiting for the birds to peck
at him and call him names.

But what did he see, as he looked down
at the water? His reflection no longer
showed an ugly grey bird.

He was dazzling white, with a long graceful neck – just like theirs.

"Hello! You're one of us."

They greeted him warmly.

Then two children came
into the garden.

"Look, there's
a beautiful
new swan!"

The young swan held his head high.
He had never dreamed that he would be this
happy, back when he was an ugly duckling.

72

The Three Billy Goats Gruff

Once there lived three billy goats gruff. They loved nothing more than eating grass all day long.

Munch!

74

Munch! Munch!
But it had to be the sweetest, tastiest grass they could find.

"Time to look for some tastier grass," said the big billy goat gruff to his brothers one day. So they set off along the river.

76

They wandered for miles and miles.
"Are we there yet?"
asked the littlest billy goat gruff.
"I'm starving!"

At last they came to a bridge, and on the other side of it they saw a lush meadow. "That looks delicious!" said the littlest billy goat gruff.

"Yummy!" agreed his brothers.

But **a nasty troll**
lived under the bridge. He had long,
sharp claws and pointed teeth. He liked
nothing better than goat for dinner.

79

Trip trap, trip trap!

"I'll cross first," said the littlest billy goat gruff. And off he trotted with a trip trap, trip trap, over the wooden bridge.

80

Suddenly the troll jumped out in front of him. "Who is trip-trapping over MY BRIDGE?" he roared.

"Only me," said the littlest billy goat gruff. "I need to get to the meadow beyond."

81

"Oh, but you should wait until my brother comes along," said the littlest billy goat gruff.

"He's FAR bigger than me."

"Byeee!"

And with a hop and a skip, the little goat jumped into the meadow beyond.

83

Not long after, the middle-sized billy goat gruff crossed the bridge. Trip trap, trip trap!

"STOP RIGHT THERE!"
the troll roared, jumping out.
"Who is trip-trapping over
MY BRIDGE?"

"It's me, looking for tasty grass to eat," said the middle-sized billy goat gruff.

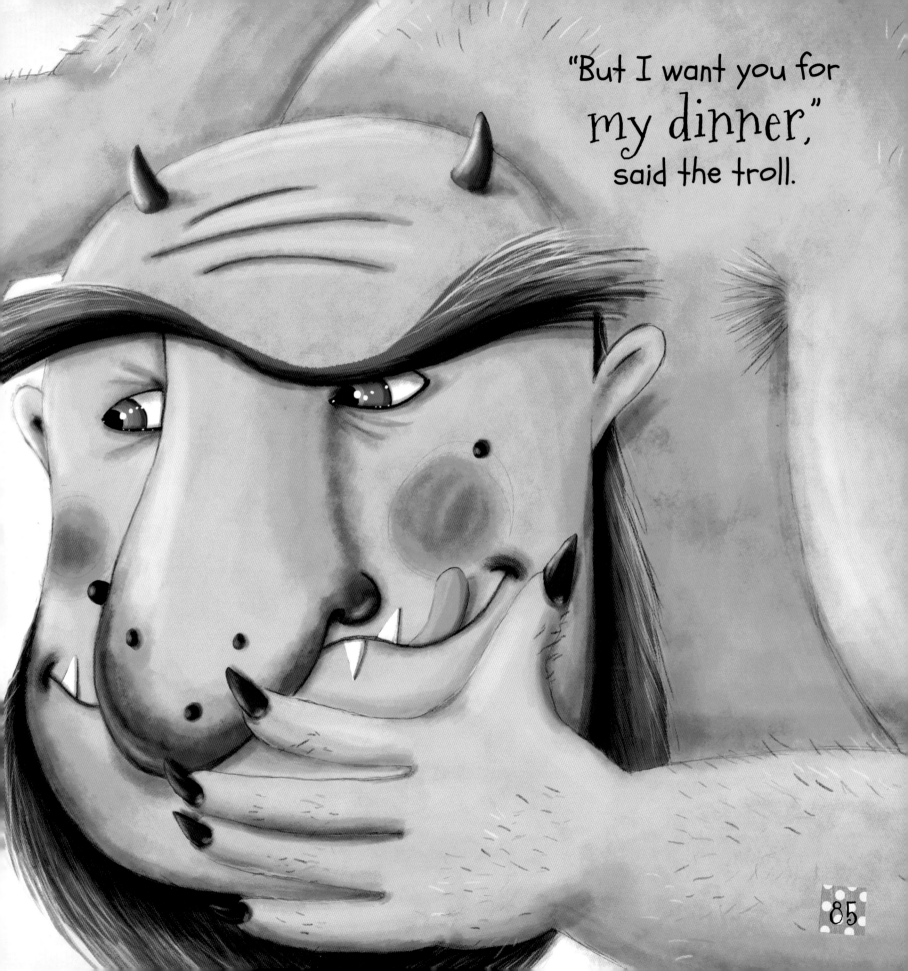

"Oh, wait for my big brother – he'll make a much better meal," said the middle-sized billy goat gruff. And with a hop and a skip, he jumped into the meadow.

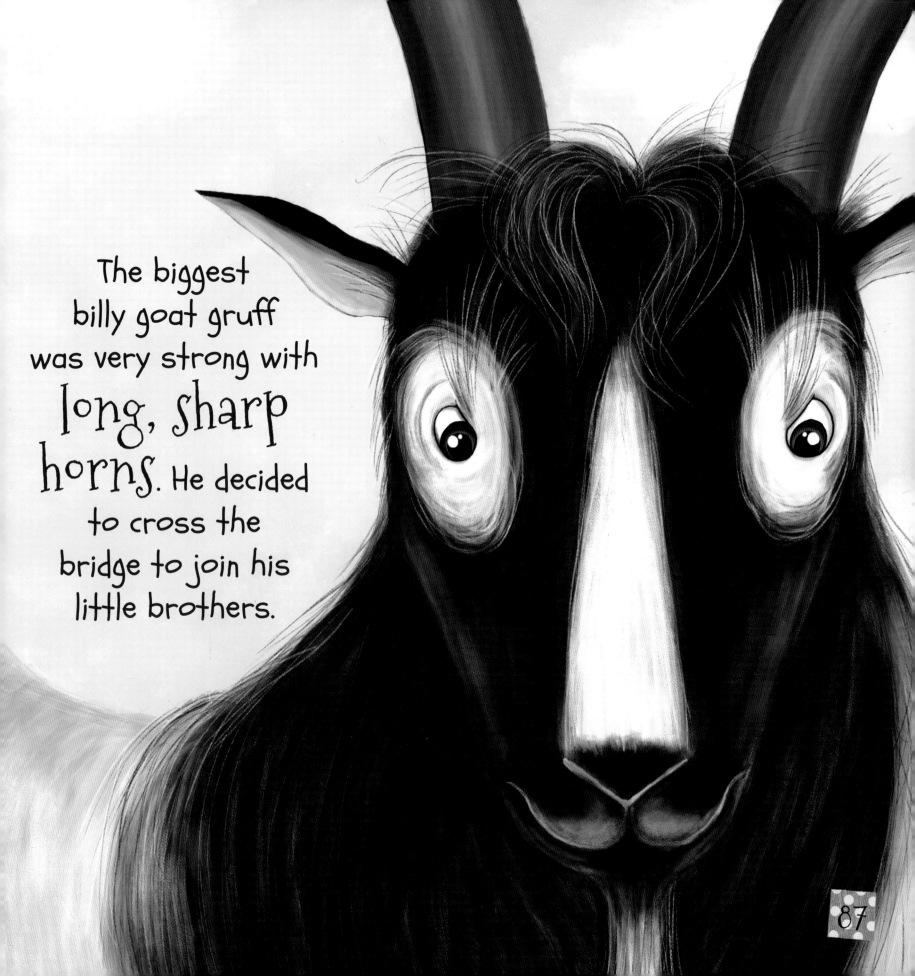

The biggest billy goat gruff was very strong with long, sharp horns. He decided to cross the bridge to join his little brothers.

TRIP
TRAP,
The big billy goat
gruff clattered over
the wooden bridge.

88

Up went the troll high into the air, over the bridge and far into the river below. SPLASH!

"ARGGGH!"

TRIP TRAP, TRIP TRAP!
The big billy goat gruff clattered all
the way over the bridge and jumped
into the meadow beyond.

95

The three billy goats gruff lived happily ever after. They were never bothered by trolls again!